Ning

ORPEN PRESS

Acknowledgements

I would like to thank the Human Givens College for recognising and encouraging my creativity. I especially thank the college principal Ivan Tyrrell and Director of Studies Joe Griffin for their inspirational teaching of the most effective and transforming psychotherapy I have learned to date.

I also thank Brenda O'Hanlon, my editor, for believing in me, working so hard and doing such a wonderful job. I am sincerely grateful to Sue Saunders for sorting out the computer and being my right hand in Ireland. Without her IT expertise and patience these stories might not have reached the publisher so promptly!

Thank you to my colleague Sue Harper for listening to my first story and telling me to "go for it", and to Pat Williams, founder-director of the London College of Storytellers, for advising me to get the stories published. Thanks also to all my colleagues and friends who have encouraged me over the years.

Of course, most importantly, I thank my incredibly supportive husband Frank, who is my best friend and my stability, and who has allowed me to remain a child at heart.

And a big thank you to all the children who have inspired me, and without whom I would not have known the healing properties of these stories.

Ning

Written by Pamela Woodford

Illustrations by Tom McMahon

ORPEN PRESS
Lonsdale House
Avoca Ave
Blackrock
Co. Dublin
Ireland

e-mail: info@orpenpress.com
www.orpenpress.com

© Pamela Woodford, 2013
ISBN: 978-1-871305-81-4

Printed in Northern Ireland by GPS Colour Graphics Ltd

Preface

STORIES HAVE ALWAYS BEEN a powerful way of conveying universal human dreams and dreads, of inspiring us to find strengths we didn't know we had, to overcome difficulties, and to flourish and grow.

Stories are particularly effective with children, as I know from my work as a consultant Human Givens psychotherapist over the past twelve years. During that time, I have told countless stories, many of which I made up myself, and I've found that the right story can get to the heart of the matter and bring about swift, positive change.

Children as young as five, but also adolescents and adults, have heard my stories, which have proved to be a key way of addressing imperative issues.

All the stories in the *Brighter Little Minds* series encourage the reader/listener to use their imagination in a positive way. There are also suggestions for activities that aim to further embed the learning and therapeutic metaphor contained in each book.

The story of *Ning* addresses such issues as: being accepted for who you are, thinking outside of the box, tackling perfectionism, autism, encouraging self-worth and individual ideas, and much more.

Suggestions for Activity:

Write your name backwards and use it for a day, e.g. Ben Ross becomes "Neb Ssor" and Kate Jones becomes "Etak Senoj".

Create your very own "thing": make whatever you decide to from lots of different bits and pieces.

THIS is the story of Ning, who you will get to know very well over the next few pages. First of all, I will let him introduce himself:

"Hello, my name is Ning, and I am very happy to meet you. You may be thinking that I am a strange-looking fellow. Well, I may look a bit different from what folk call 'normal', but I am very friendly, with a huge heart, and the question mark above my head means I have an inquisitive, intelligent mind, which I use to help me with my problems. I will keep you guessing for the moment as to what is in my brown box."

Ning. What a funny word! Not ping, ring or sing, but Ning. Let's find out some more about Ning.

Ning just loves turning things around. In fact, he even did this with his own name. He gave himself the full name of Ning-Tur, when really his name is Tur-Ning, which, when said quickly, is like the word "turning". You know, like going along the street and then *turning* a corner into another street; turning around when you dance; or even turning around to see what's behind you. Sometimes it can be like turning a page over in a book and seeing new words or pictures. And other times it can be like turning a blank page into your very own picture.

No wonder Ning liked to turn things around with a name like that!

Ning had learned that turning things around was a very interesting thing to be able to do. What's more, it was fun. It was like looking at things from different angles and from different directions.

Ning had even turned his age around.

You see, he was really 80 years old, which is an 8 followed by a 0. But Ning put the 0 before the 8 so that he became only 8 years old.

"After all," he thought, "it's much more fun being 8." In fact, he could turn his age around to any age he wanted to be.

When Ning was turning things around, he would turn things inside out, back to front and upside down.

Some days he would put his tee shirt on back to front with the label poking out, saying: "Dry clean only. This garment might shrink." Pretending that the label was a part of him was a good way for Ning to have some fun and try to get out of having a bath.

Other days he would put his coat on back to front and strut about with his arms all stiff in front of him like a robot!

And when he was feeling in a playful mood, but brave and full of energy too, Ning would turn himself upside down and try to walk along on his hands, or even on his head instead of his feet!

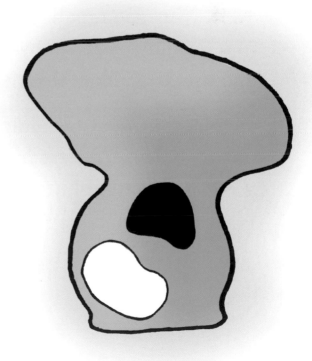

But this usually ended up with Ning laughing so much that he would tumble about on the floor, rolling over and over and getting the hiccups! "Hic, hic!" Then he would have a drink of water and drink it from the opposite side of the glass, standing upside down and holding his nose! Oh, Ning-Tur, whatever next?

Well, Ning soon realised that he could turn a gloomy day into a sunny one, just by forgetting about the grey clouds and thinking about the bright, golden sun.

He could turn a frown into a smile, just by putting the frown upside down. "You try it," Ning said. And so I tried. I made a frown, and then I turned it upside down ... and it worked – I smiled!

Sometimes Ning would look into the mirror and practise turning his face around from a frown to a smile. In fact, he would see how many different shapes his face could make, but somehow he would always end up turning his face into a smile.

As you can see, Ning liked to be happy, and he always tried to make the best of things. He learned that he had the ability to turn things around so that they could be so much better. He loved letting his imagination work.

One day, when Ning was sitting comfortably with his own thoughts, he imagined a large, plain cardboard box.

There was no clue as to what was in it or no instructions with it. In fact, it seemed a very ordinary cardboard box ... except for one thing – it seemed to be alive ... it was moving around the floor!

"How strange," thought Ning, wanting to explore and find out more.

He looked at the box from one side and then from the other and realised that it was actually upside down.

Then Ning very carefully turned the box over and noticed that it didn't have a lid.

That is because a lid should never be put on anything that is moving and growing. And, yes, believe it or not, this box was doing just that – it was moving and growing.

Inside there were all sorts of shapes trying to find their way out.

The first things to come out of the box were cones, some as small as ice cream cones and others as big as traffic cones, all looking around and seeing what was about.

Then out came some metal rods, very strong and straight. After that came wooden planks, some wide enough to walk along and others just narrow enough to balance upon.

And then there were corner pieces, nuts and bolts, and nails and screws all ready to join things together. All the different parts were moving about doing their own little jobs, whilst growing into something grand.

And it seemed a very
short time before ...
there it was
– the most fascinating
climbing frame
Ning had ever
seen.

By this time he was almost exploding with excitement at the thought of trying it out.

And so he began to climb up and down the climbing frame, and in and out, finding his own way of getting around it.

He would roll over on
the rods ...

and balance on the planks.

14

And he would pull himself around the corners.

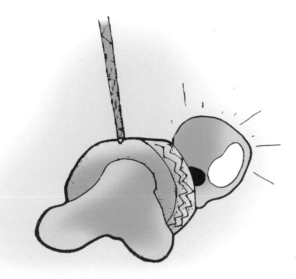

Sometimes it was hard going as Ning tried to climb to the top, and other times he even got stuck.

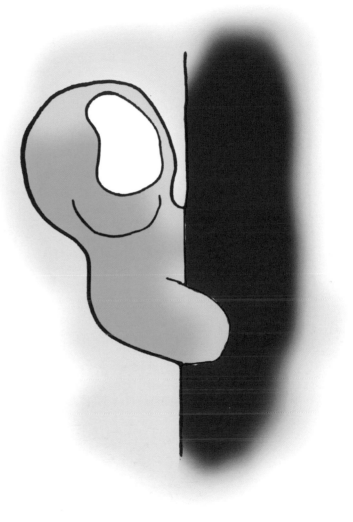

15

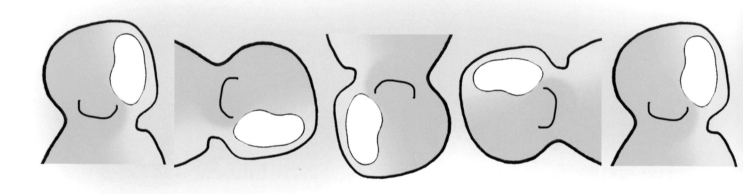

But, of course, Ning, being Ning-Tur, would just turn himself around, upside down and inside out, and see things from all different angles.

It was then that Ning realised it didn't matter if he reached the top or not – it was much more fun and interesting to explore.

And so it was that Ning-Tur just kept on turning ... and smiling ... and turning ... and learning. And he's wondering what you will learn about turning ... and smiling ... and turning ... and learning. Perhaps you'll tell him sometime.

THE END

Ning